WHY DID HE DIE?

By Audrey Harris

Illustrated by Susan Salladé Dalke

Published by

Lerner Publications Company

Minneapolis, Minnesota

Published simultaneously in Canada by
J. M. Dent & Sons, Ltd., Don Mills, Ontario

Library of Congress Catalog Card Number: 65-22217

Second Printing 1967
Third Printing 1968

FOREWORD

The subject of death is an unusual one for a children's book. Our natural reluctance to discuss this matter, even as adults, takes on added uneasiness when the topic is raised by a child. How can we explain what death is? As adults we do not so much understand death, as gain the courage to confront it. Yet children, even the youngest, experience the deprivation of loved ones by death. They ask what it means. We felt that this poem, representing one mother's heartfelt effort to speak to her child, deserved publication and should be brought to a wider public.

The Editors
Lerner Publications Company

Scott went out to call for Jim,
But came home right away.
Jim had lots of company;
He could not come to play.

"Jimmy's house is very sad,
And Jimmy's mother cried.
They said his Granddad passed away,
Does that mean that he died?"

Scott's mother sat down next to him,
And said that this was true.
Scott asked a lot of questions then,
Mother answered all she knew.

"Jim's Granddad was an old, old man,
He was very, very sick.
His heart was very tired,
And could no longer tick.

"All things,
machines,
plants,
animals,
And human beings, too,
Rust,
or decay,
or die
and pass away.
These changes happen all the time,
All life flows on, it cannot stay.

"Do you remember, Scott, last fall?
The leaves flew down,
the year was getting old,
Summer turned to fall,
and fall to wintertime,
Green leafy branches turned to brown
and then were bare and cold.

"The leaves soon wrinkled on the ground
and died,
But in the spring new leaves
will come to grow
on that same tree
where now you have
your swing.
New grass will rise from the earth,
New flowers bloom from the cold,
hard dirt.

"And, Scott, remember Tag, our dog?
And the bedroom slippers that he tore?
He died because he was too old,
His heart could beat no more.

"There's a motor in your father's car
That makes the auto go.
When the motor gets worn out
Then the car can't run, you know.

"The heart is like this motor,
If it stops, then it is dead.
Old, old people must someday die.
New little babies are born instead.

"Just think, if people lived forever
How crowded all the earth would be.
Birthday cakes would have thousands of candles,
People would have to live in the sea."

"Will you and Father die soon?"
Scott saw his mother smile.
"No, not 'til you're an old, old man
We'll live a long, long while."

"You said that old, old people die,
But I know a girl named Mae
Who said her little sister
Was sick and passed away."

Mother said, "Once in awhile
It's true some children die.
But not often, I'm happy to say,
And I will tell you why.

“Some motors die in brand new cars —
And some children are not strong.
Their hearts won’t beat ’til they are old
They just can’t live too long.

“Once in awhile, a child might die
But not very often, you see.
And you, my Scott, will grow as strong
As a giant, giant tall oak tree.

"The important thing to remember
Is not how long we live.
It's how nice we are to others,
And the happiness that we give.

"A short poem may be as beautiful
As the long, long story we read.
If we're kind and thoughtful as long as we live,
That's the right kind of life to lead."

"Is Jimmy's Granddad dead for good?
Can the motor use some glue?
Will the doctor fix him up?
To be as good as new?"

"No, Scott, he's never coming back,
That's what the doctor said.
His body changed when he got old —
That part of him is dead.

"But the thing that Jim remembers —
His kindness, love, and cheer —
Those memories will never die,
These thoughts bring Granddad near."

"Why is Jimmy very sad?
He knows old people die.
His Granddad was so jolly —
Why does he have to cry?"

"To lose what we love, and can never get back
Leaves us with a painful sore,
It's hard to think his Granddad's gone —
Jim won't see him any more."

“If he is dead and cannot move,
Is he buried in the ground?”
“They place him in a sort of box
With flowers all around.

"In a cemetery park
Jim's Granddad has a space,
With plants and trees and flowers —
With God — there is his place."

Jim just called and asked if he
Could come and spend the day.
He won't forget his Granddad,
But now it's time to play!

ABOUT THE AUTHOR

Audrey Harris was born in Chicago, Illinois. She studied drama at the Goodman Theatre and later took a degree in speech correction at the University of Michigan. She is planning graduate work in this field at DePaul University. Her professional positions have been as a speech therapist, audiologist and a teacher of drama. She has combined this with an active interest in repertory theatre acting, writing, and leading a Junior Great Books course. She has two children. The Harris family lives in Chicago.

ABOUT THE ARTIST

Susan Salladé Dalke was born in Reading, Pennsylvania. She earned a Bachelor of Fine Arts degree in illustration at the Rhode Island School of Design. She is a member of the Minnetonka Center of Arts and Education and a lecturer at the Walker Art Center in Minneapolis. She has done television art work and taught privately. Her painting is devoted primarily to landscapes, still lifes and animal portraiture. Mr. and Mrs. Stuart Dalke reside in Minnetonka, Minnesota.